THE MUD CRUSTS

SABRE-TOOTHED TERRORS

Damian Harvey
Illustrated by Ned Joliffe

A & C Black • London

Chapter ONE

Icy, cold water dripped onto Lowbrow Mudcrust's neck and slowly trickled down his back. He shivered and moved away from the wall. Somehow, he'd managed to find the only part of Chief Hawknose's cave where the roof leaked. But at least he got a bit of peace and quiet there.

Ever since their hut had sunk into the mud of Slimepool Swamp, the Mudcrusts had been living with the Hawknose family in their cave at the bottom of Icecap Mountain. They'd only planned to stay for a night, but one night had grown

7

into two, and two nights had stretched into a week.

They were waiting for the heavy rains to stop so they could move into a cave of their own. Chief Hawknose had admitted there was one further up the mountain. But Lowbrow's wife, Flora, refused to go while it was still raining. And her sister, Fauna, had insisted they stay until the weather improved.

The sisters were having a great time – chatting and swapping recipes for mammoth burgers and roasted boar. Even Lowbrow's sons, Bogweed and Fungus were having fun. Bogweed spent his time making hand-print pictures on the wall with his cousin, Mere. And when Fungus wasn't busy teasing his brother, he spent *his* time lazing by the fire.

8

Taking their best hunting spears, Lowbrow and Chief Hawknose left the cave and stomped off towards the forest in silence. The heavy rain had turned the path into a mudslide, and the two men were soaking wet and filthy by the time they reached the shelter of the trees.

"Why did you want to go hunting?" complained Chief Hawknose. "We could be sitting by the fire now, keeping nice and warm."

"Don't blame *me*," said Lowbrow. "*I* didn't ask you to come." He stopped to examine some animal tracks in the mud, then pointed to one of the paths that snaked its way into the trees. "Wild boar," he said. "It went that way."

They had hardly gone any distance, when something ran across the path

in front of them. They just caught sight of a long tail before it disappeared into the bushes.

"What was *that*?" asked Chief Hawknose.

Lowbrow shrugged. "I'm not sure," he said. "But it was big."

"Perhaps it's a wild boar," said Chief Hawknose, nodding his head excitedly.

"Wild boar don't have tails like that," said Lowbrow with a frown. "It looked a bit like a –"

A low growling noise made Lowbrow's mouth snap shut and his eyes open wide. Something was moving in the bushes close by. He looked at Chief Hawknose and pointed upwards.

Chief Hawknose nodded, then they both moved quickly.

Dropping their spears, they scrambled up the nearest tree. At the same time, a large shape exploded out of the bushes behind them. Lowbrow felt a sharp pain in his leg and lost his grip on the branch he was holding. As he started to fall, Chief Hawknose grabbed his arm and pulled him up into the tree.

There was a deep scratch on Lowbrow's leg where a savage claw had caught him, and a trickle of blood ran down his foot.

"That was close," said Chief Hawknose. "It's a good job I was here to look after you."

Lowbrow scowled, but didn't say anything. Instead, he held tightly onto the branches and peered down at their attacker.

The creature glared back with fierce, yellow eyes. Two long canine teeth hung below its chin like the fangs of a giant snake, and its lips were pulled back in a vicious snarl.

"I've not seen a sabre-toothed tiger around here for years," said Chief Hawknose.

"I'd *hoped* I would never see one again," said Lowbrow, rubbing his leg.

Below them, the tiger let out a loud roar and sprang at the tree. Its huge claws sank into the trunk and shredded the bark, but it couldn't quite climb up.

Lowbrow shuffled further along the branch, wishing he hadn't dropped his hunting spear.

The sabre-toothed tiger was prowling around the bottom of the tree, growling, as it looked for an easier way up. Then something caught its attention. A small boar had come trotting along the forest path with its nose to the ground. It hadn't noticed Lowbrow and Chief Hawknose, or the sabre-toothed tiger. But the tiger spotted the boar straight away.

With a snarl, the great beast pounced. The tiger sank its huge teeth into the stunned creature before it knew what was happening. The boar let out a squeal and struggled to get away, but it didn't have a chance.

"Hey!" cried Chief Hawknose. "That was going to be our dinner."

The tiger dragged the boar into the bushes and began tearing apart its prey.

Lowbrow shook his head sadly. "It could have been worse," he said. "*We* could have been the tiger's dinner." He shivered. Hunting was always dangerous but that had been *too* close.

"Don't worry," laughed Chief Hawknose. "I won't tell anyone that the big brave hunter got chased up a tree by a little pussycat."

"Good!" hissed Lowbrow. "And I won't tell anyone that the great Chief Hawknose had to hide in the tree, either."

The two men glared at each other in silence, and waited until the sounds of eating had died away. Eventually, all they could hear was the patter of rain on the leaves and the distant howling and roaring of other beasts deep in the forest.

"Do you think it's gone?" whispered Chief Hawknose.

Lowbrow shrugged, but he didn't say a word. His leg was stinging, his bottom was sore, and he was freezing cold. They had been sitting in the tree for ages.

"I can't see anything moving," Chief Hawknose went on. "It must have gone."

Lowbrow looked around. He couldn't see anything moving, either, but it was hard to be sure. It was gloomy in the forest, and the floor was a tangle of bushes and shrubs. *Anything* could be down there.

"It's getting late," said Chief Hawknose, starting to panic. "We should get back to the cave."

Lowbrow looked up at the darkening sky and nodded. They *should* be getting back. Spending the night in a tree would be bad enough, but being stuck up there with Bignose would be unbearable — especially now that the chief had saved his life.

Chapter Two

It was dark when Lowbrow and Chief Hawknose arrived home, and Flora and Fauna were not happy.

"Where have you been?" asked Fauna. "You've been gone *ages*."

"And where's dinner?" asked Flora. "I thought you were going hunting."

"We *have* been hunting," said Lowbrow. "But we didn't catch anything."

"What about the fruit and nuts?" asked Fauna.

Lowbrow and Chief Hawknose looked at each other.

"Don't say you forgot the fruit and nuts?" said Flora.

They *had* forgotten the fruit and nuts. After climbing down from the tree, the only thing either of them had thought about was getting back to the cave. They had even forgotten to pick up their hunting spears.

"Of course we didn't forget them, dear," said Chief Hawknose. "We –"

"You *what*?" snapped his wife. "And this had better be good."

The two sisters stood side by side with their arms folded. Lowbrow thought they looked more frightening than the sabre-toothed tiger. And this time there was no tree for them to hide in.

"We were attacked," said Lowbrow.

"*Attacked*?" said Flora.

"Yes," said Chief Hawknose. "By a sabre-toothed tiger."

"A whole family of them," said Lowbrow, trying to make it sound even more terrible than it was. "Look – one of them nearly had me." He showed them the scratch on his leg. It wasn't bleeding any more, but it still looked very sore.

"Cool," said Fungus, coming over to see what all the fuss was about.

Bogweed joined his brother and pulled a face when he saw the scratch. "How did you escape from a whole family of sabre-toothed tigers?" he asked.

"We had to fight them off," said Chief Hawknose.

"They growled and snarled and gnashed their huge teeth," said Lowbrow.

"They even broke our hunting spears," added Chief Hawknose.

"So we had to use all the fruit and nuts we'd gathered," said Lowbrow.

"Fruit and nuts!" said Mere, from the other side of the cave. "How did you fight sabre-toothed tigers with fruit and nuts?"

"We threw them," said Chief Hawknose, nodding to his daughter.

"They didn't like that," said Lowbrow. "You should have seen them run."

The two sisters listened to all this, amazed. They were both starting to feel a bit guilty about being so cross.

"Why don't you come and sit by the fire," said Fauna. "You must be freezing."

"Yes," said Flora. "Put your feet up. I'm sure we can find something to eat."

So while Flora and Fauna made supper from the last of their food, Lowbrow and Chief Hawknose sat in front of the fire and relaxed.

All Lowbrow wanted to do was close his eyes and go to sleep, but Bogweed, Fungus and Mere wanted to hear more about the sabre-toothed tigers.

"How big were their fangs?" asked Bogweed.

"Did you stab them with your spears?" asked Fungus.

"Weren't you frightened?" asked Mere.

So Lowbrow and Chief Hawknose repeated the story about how they had bravely defeated the vicious sabre-toothed tigers and sent then running into the forest. But neither of them mentioned the hours they had spent hiding in the tree.

The next morning, Lowbrow was woken by a deep growling sound.

He opened his eyes and found himself staring straight into the open jaws of a sabre-toothed tiger.

"AARGH!" he yelled, and fell off his rock with a heavy thud.

The cave filled with laughter and Lowbrow turned bright red as he picked himself up and found everyone looking

at him. Fungus was holding an old
sabre-toothed tiger skull in his hands
and was moving the bottom jaw up and
down as he growled and roared.

"We found it further up the mountain,"
he said. "Cool, isn't it?"

Lowbrow stared wide-eyed at the old
tiger skull and nodded slowly. He could
feel his heart pounding and sweat had
started to pour down his face.

"You shouldn't frighten your old dad like that," said Chief Hawknose. "He's not as young as he was."

Lowbrow scowled at Chief Hawknose and opened his mouth to reply – he wasn't going to let old Bignose poke fun at him, even if he *had* saved his life – but before he managed to say anything, Flora spoke.

"It's stopped raining," she announced. "I think it's time to move into that cave."

"Good idea," said her sister. "Hawkie will show you the way."

"I'll come with you, too," said Mere.

"You can go later," said her mother. "I need your help here."

While the Mudcrusts gathered their bits and pieces together, Chief Hawknose grumbled and complained.

"Come on," he said. "I haven't got all day. There's important work for me to do."

Lowbrow ground his teeth together but managed to stop himself from saying anything. The sooner they moved into this other cave, the better. He'd had enough of Chief Bignose to last him a lifetime.

Chapter THREE

The cave was higher up the mountain, not far from where the Hawknoses lived, and it didn't take long to get there. Its entrance was hidden from view by a clump of trees. Standing in front, you could see the forest stretching out below, and the path that wound its way through Slimepool Swamp towards the river. In the distance you could even see the mouth of the valley.

"Well," said Chief Hawknose. "Here we are. It's not as nice as our cave, of course, but it's better than nothing."

"It looks wonderful," said Flora, admiring the view. "I'm sure it will be fine."

Bogweed carefully put down the wooden bowls he had been carrying and poked his head inside the cave.

"It smells a bit funny," he said, pulling a face.

"Don't worry about that," said Flora. "We'll soon have it cleaned out."

Lowbrow and Fungus had been carrying a rolled-up mammoth fur between them. They dropped it onto the floor as soon as they reached the cave.

"Phew," said Fungus. "That's as heavy as a pile of rocks."

"And it's soggy," complained Lowbrow.

"It will make a nice rug when it's dry," said Flora. "This mammoth fur belonged to my mother."

Lowbrow knew better than to say anything else. Instead, he walked into the cave to have a good look round.

"It's full of old bones," he said.

"That doesn't matter," said Flora. "Come on – as soon as we get it cleaned out, we can move in properly."

30

Bogweed cut some soft branches from a bush and tied them together with a piece of vine. "It's a sweeping bush," he explained, and started clearing up some of the animal bones that were scattered around on the floor.

The cave was a lot bigger than it looked, and it took quite a while to get it cleaned out. But it didn't take long to discover where the funny smell was coming from.

Bogweed was sweeping together a large pile of bones when there was a crunch, a meaty squelch, then –

"YUCK!" he cried. "What was *that*?"

"You wet wimp," said Fungus, looking at the floor. "It's only a wild boar."

"Is it dead?" asked Bogweed.

"I hope so," said Fungus. "There's only

half of it left. It looks like something's been eating it."

Bogweed dragged the remains of the boar towards the mouth of the cave and dropped it on the pile of bones he'd swept together.

"It's starting to rain again," he said. "I'll get rid of it properly when it's stopped."

"Bring the mammoth fur inside," said Flora. "I don't want it getting any wetter than it already is."

Lowbrow and Fungus dragged the wet, smelly mammoth fur inside while Flora and Bogweed set out the wooden bowls in front of the cave to catch some of the rainwater. When they'd finished, the Mudcrusts sat down together in their new home.

"I think I'm going to like it here," said Flora, happily.

Lowbrow didn't say anything. He was upset about losing their mud hut. But he had to admit, having a cave of their own wasn't too bad – it was nice and dry and there was much more space.

Suddenly, a strange growling noise filled the air.

"What was that?" said Bogweed, looking towards the mouth of the cave.

"It was me," said Fungus, rubbing his belly. "I'm starving."

"So am I," agreed Bogweed.

"I'll go and catch something for dinner," said Lowbrow. "It looks like the rain has stopped."

"Good idea," said Flora. "But keep your eyes open for that tiger."

Lowbrow was just getting to his feet when there was another growling sound.

"You'd better be quick," laughed Flora. "Fungus's stomach is really complaining now."

"That wasn't my stomach," said Fungus, looking worried. "That noise came from outside."

Lowbrow froze and stared at the

mouth of the cave. The light from the watery sun was casting a strange shadow against one of the walls.

"Hide!" he whispered, urgently.

"What is it?" asked Flora.

Lowbrow pressed a finger to his lips and steered everyone further inside.

As they looked for somewhere to hide, the shadow became clearer and Bogweed's eyes opened wide with fear. "It's a sabre-toothed tiger," he whispered.

Lowbrow looked around frantically, but it was no use. There was nowhere safe to go and all their hunting spears were still outside.

"Here!" whispered Bogweed.

He had crawled under the mammoth fur and was holding up one edge so they could all get underneath.

"Come on," he whispered, and as quickly and quietly as they could, the other Mudcrusts squeezed in beside him.

Lowbrow managed to cover his legs just as the sabre-toothed tiger appeared at the mouth of the cave.

Chapter FOUR

The tiger sniffed the air. Then it lowered its head and started sniffing the ground.

"What's it doing?" whispered Lowbrow.

Bogweed had one eye pressed against a small hole in the mammoth fur, and could just see what was happening.

"I don't know," he replied. "It seems to just be sniffing things at the moment."

"If it sniffs *us* out, it will have us for dinner," said Lowbrow.

Bogweed watched as the great beast padded around near the mouth of the cave, sniffing and snuffling the ground.

"I think it's found the wild boar," he whispered.

From where they lay, the Mudcrusts could hear the sabre-toothed tiger tearing at the remains of the wild boar they'd found earlier.

"Perhaps it will go away when it's finished eating," Fungus suggested.

Lowbrow nodded. "I hope so," he said. "But until it does, nobody move."

That wasn't as easy as it sounded. The cave floor was hard and lumpy, and the wet, smelly mammoth fur was quite heavy. As time went on, it started getting very warm under there, too.

The Mudcrusts felt like they'd been hiding for ages. Lowbrow's back was starting to ache, Flora was getting pins and needles in her arm, Bogweed's nose

tickled every time he breathed in, and Fungus had nodded off and was starting to snore.

Bogweed peeped through the hole in the mammoth fur again to see what the sabre-toothed tiger was doing. Like Fungus, the tiger seemed to have fallen asleep. It was lying on its side at the entrance to the cave with the remains of the half-eaten boar still clamped between its huge teeth.

It was getting hotter and hotter beneath the fur. Bogweed could feel beads of sweat running down his face, and his tickly nose was getting worse. He tried rubbing it with his hand, but it was really starting to annoy him. It was tickling more than ever and he felt sure he was going to –

The sneeze erupted from his mouth and echoed around the cave.

"Ssh!" hissed Lowbrow and Flora, together.

"Be quiet," moaned Fungus, and gave Bogweed a punch on the arm. "I was trying to sleep."

"Ouch!" cried Bogweed.

"Silence!" hissed Flora. "The pair of you."

But it was too late. The sabre-toothed tiger had already heard them. It dropped the half-eaten boar it had been gnawing and sprang to its feet. The great beast lowered its head, let out a low growl and stepped into the cave.

"What's it doing?" whispered Lowbrow.

Bogweed froze. He could feel the hairs on the back of his neck standing on end.

"It's ... it's ... it's coming towards us," he stammered.

The sabre-toothed tiger let out another low growl that seemed to make the rock beneath them tremble.

Bogweed watched as it padded towards where they were hiding. It opened its mouth in a vicious snarl, then leapt forwards. Bogweed closed his eyes tightly and felt the tiger's heavy paws land on the edge of the mammoth fur. He waited for its savage claws to rip through it... But nothing happened. The great beast let out a snort and was gone.

Bogweed poked his head out from their hiding place and stared in amazement. There was no sign of the tiger anywhere, but Mere was standing with her back to the cave wall, her face as pale as ice. In her arms was a large bowl of nuts and berries.

"What are *you* doing here?" asked Bogweed. "And where's that sabre-toothed tiger?"

"Mum said I should bring this round," explained Mere. "But when I arrived, I saw the tiger charging out. It looked terrified."

"I think this cave belongs to the tiger," said Flora.

"That explains all the bones we found," said Bogweed. "The tiger must use the cave to store its food. It catches something, eats part of it, then brings the rest here for later."

"Never mind," said Mere. "You've frightened it off now."

"*We* didn't frighten it off," said Bogweed. "*We* were hiding."

Lowbrow coughed loudly as he crawled out from the mammoth fur.

He didn't want old Bignose to hear about this. "Mudcrusts *never* hide," he said. "We were just waiting for the right time to chase it away."

"Well, it's gone now," said Flora. "So *we* can get on with moving into our new home."

"What do you mean?" said Lowbrow, suddenly forgetting to be brave. "We can't stay here. This cave belongs to the sabre-toothed tiger. It'll be back soon."

"We are staying *right* here," insisted Flora Mudcrust. "I'm not letting some big-toothed pussycat chase us out of our lovely new home."

"But what else can we do, my dear?" asked Lowbrow. "We can't share the cave with a tiger."

"No, we can't," said Flora. "*You'll* have to get rid of it."

"But –"

"No buts," said Flora, firmly. "If you and Chief Hawknose managed to chase off a whole family with just a handful of fruit and nuts, I'm sure you and Fungus will have no trouble getting rid of this one."

Lowbrow was beginning to wish he had never made up the story about his meeting with the tigers, but it was too late for that.

"Right," he said, with a frown. "We'd better get going then."

"It will be dark soon," said Flora. "And Mere has brought this food for our dinner. It can wait until tomorrow."

"But the tiger might come back here in the middle of the night," said Lowbrow.

"It might," agreed Flora. "So I want you and Fungus here to protect us if it does. Mere had better stay, too. It's not safe for her to walk home."

"I'll make a fire," suggested Bogweed, gathering some sticks and dry leaves. "That should help keep the tiger away."

It wasn't long before there was a

small blaze burning in front of the cave and the Mudcrusts had settled down for the night. While the rest of them slept, Lowbrow sat staring into the darkness, looking for any sign of movement.

Early the next morning, Lowbrow and Fungus grabbed a couple of hunting spears before setting off in search of the sabre-toothed tiger.

"Remember," said Flora, "you're just trying to frighten it off. Sabre-toothed tigers can be very nasty."

"Don't worry," said Fungus, bravely. "We'll sort it out. And we'll catch something tasty for supper, too."

Flora, Bogweed and Mere waved as Lowbrow and his eldest son set off down the mountain towards the forest.

"I hope they'll be all right," said Mere.

"So do I," said Bogweed, remembering the trouble they'd had trying to catch a wild boar back in the swamp. "Fungus isn't the best hunter in the world."

"Neither is your dad," said Flora. "That's why I had to send them away for the day. Now – how are we going to get rid of that sabre-toothed terror?"

Chapter FIVE

Bogweed splashed water onto his arms and face, then shivered. The stream ran down from the top of Icecap Mountain and it was freezing cold. He really missed the nice hot spring water of his pong pit near the swamp, but he was determined to wash off some of the terrible mammoth smell that was clinging to him.

It stank!

As he walked back to their cave, Bogweed tried to think of how they could get rid of the sabre-toothed tiger. Killing it would be difficult. They would need

lots of hunters and it would be very dangerous. It would definitely be easier to frighten it off – but how? Something had scared the sabre-toothed tiger last night, but it wouldn't be long before it came back, and this time they might not be so lucky. This time they would have to make sure it left for good.

As he got closer to the cave, Bogweed heard a strange wailing sound and his heart almost missed a beat.

Something was walking out of their cave. Something big and brown.

Bogweed crouched behind a rock and tried to work out what it was. Just for a moment, he actually thought it was a mammoth – and the sound he'd heard had been just like a mammoth's call. But mammoths didn't shuffle in quite

that way, and they certainly didn't drag half of their fur behind them.

The wet, smelly mammoth fur crumpled to the ground and Flora and Mere crawled out from beneath it.

"Pooh!" complained Mere. "That thing stinks."

Bogweed laughed and came out from behind his rock. "I know," he agreed. "It smells just like a wet, woolly mammoth. And you *looked* just like a mammoth for a moment."

"We were just bringing it out here to dry," said Flora.

"Well, you've just given me an idea," said Bogweed, thoughtfully.

Lowbrow and Fungus sat in the tree and watched the family of sabre-toothed tigers noisily crunching and chewing their food.

Fungus was surprised how sharp the tiger cub's teeth were, and how easily it tore through the deer they had caught. He had decided that he was never going to come into the forest again, even if

his dad *was* with him. There were too many strange creatures in the forest and too many places for them to hide. It gave him the creeps.

It took a long time for the sabre-toothed tigers to move off – and when they did, they took the half-eaten deer with them.

"They'll save that for later," said Lowbrow.

Fungus nodded. "Where will they keep it?" he asked.

Lowbrow frowned for a moment before answering. "Probably in a cave," he replied. Then his eyes opened wide as he realised what he'd just said. He scrambled to the ground and grabbed his spear before charging off, back towards their home. "Come on!" he shouted.

Fungus didn't need telling twice. There was no way he was staying in the forest on his own.

It had taken most of the morning for Bogweed, Mere and Flora to gather enough branches and tree trunks. It had been hard work and the afternoon's task was no easier. Mere and Flora had used sharp stones to cut the pieces of wood into shape, and Bogweed had fastened them together with lengths of vine to make a large frame.

The sun was getting low when they finally stood back to admire their work.

"Not bad," said Bogweed. "Let's try it with the fur."

Together, the three of them heaved the heavy mammoth fur onto the wooden frame, then pushed and pulled it into position.

"Well, it certainly *smells* like a mammoth," said Bogweed, rubbing his nose.

"It doesn't look quite right though," said Flora. "It hasn't got any tusks."

"Will these will do?" said Mere, putting two long, curved branches where the mammoth's tusks would be.

55

The branches rested on the floor, but Bogweed thought they were just the thing. "That's perfect," he said.

"Now what do we do?" asked Mere.

"We wait," said Bogweed. "And hope it works."

The three of them moved back into the shadows of the cave and sat down, but they didn't have to sit for long. As the sun began to set, a shadow started to creep across the floor and a low growling sound came from outside.

Flora, Bogweed and Mere huddled together at the back of the cave and held their breath. They tried to keep as quiet and still as they could, but Bogweed couldn't stop himself from trembling. If the tiger came inside, it would see them straight away, and this time they

didn't have the old mammoth fur to hide beneath.

The sabre-toothed tiger appeared near the mouth of the cave and dropped the half-eaten deer onto the floor. It carefully padded round the mammoth shape, gave it a sniff, then stepped out of sight with a growl.

Bogweed breathed a sigh of relief, but none of them moved. The danger wasn't over yet.

After a few minutes, the sabre-toothed tiger was back, sniffing at the ground near the huge mammoth shape again. It let out another growl and pawed at the edge of the fur.

"It's not going to work," whispered Bogweed, sounding worried. He was sure the smell of the mammoth fur had frightened the tiger the night before, but this time it was going to need something else. He couldn't think what.

Suddenly, Mere jumped to her feet.

The sabre-toothed tiger spotted the movement straight away and sprang back from the cave mouth, glaring inside to see what it was. It bared its teeth and

snarled, then Mere opened her mouth and let out a howling, wailing cry. It echoed round the cave and Bogweed had to cover his ears. The noise was deafening. It sounded just like a mammoth's call.

The sabre-toothed tiger let out a yowling screech, and ran.

Mere, Bogweed and Flora hurried to the entrance of the cave just in time to see the sabre-toothed tiger disappearing into the forest.

"It won't be coming back here in a hurry," said Bogweed, happily.

"Not now it thinks there's a mammoth living in the cave," agreed Mere.

"Bogweed, you're brilliant!" said Flora.

"It wasn't *just* me," said Bogweed. "Mere's mammoth call did the trick."

"You might be right," said Flora. "But I think we should keep your homemade mammoth here for a bit longer. Just in case."

As they took Mere back to the Hawknose's cave, she showed Bogweed how to call like a mammoth. But although Bogweed practised all the way home, he still couldn't do it as well as she could.

It was dark when Lowbrow and Fungus returned, and they didn't notice the huge mammoth shape in front of the cave.

"Did you find that sabre-toothed tiger?" asked Flora, innocently.

"We ran into a whole family of them," said Lowbrow. "And they ate the deer we'd caught for dinner."

"We even heard a mammoth," said

Fungus. "I wanted to catch it but Dad said we had to come home."

"I'm surprised you didn't walk into it," said Flora. "It's standing just over there."

Lowbrow and Fungus could hardly believe their eyes when they saw the huge mammoth outside he cave.

"I don't know how you expect to *catch* a mammoth when you can't even *see* one that's standing still," laughed Bogweed.

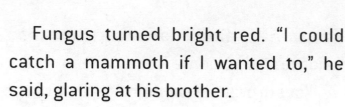

Fungus turned bright red. "I could catch a mammoth if I wanted to," he said, glaring at his brother.

"Never mind about that," said Flora. "At least we've got some deer for supper."

"Deer?" said Lowbrow. "Where did you get that from?"

"It was just lying around," said Bogweed. Then he told them about how they had made the mammoth and frightened off the sabre-toothed tiger.

Flora nodded. "See," she said. "Hunting isn't just about using spears. You have to work together and use your *brains*."

Lowbrow nodded quietly. He was too tired to feel embarrassed. He was just glad they had got rid of the sabre-toothed tiger in the end. Besides, the deer meat was tasty, and he was happy not to have Chief Hawknose bothering him any more.

Flora was happy, too, and couldn't help smiling. They finally had a cave of their own and she'd soon have it just the way she wanted. Things seemed to be looking up for the Mudcrusts at last.

Bogweed was thinking how well everything had turned out, too. His mother was right, hunting *wasn't* just about using spears, it was also about using your brain. And that was something *he* was good at. He loved being

able to picture things in his head and then make them, like they'd done with the mammoth.

Only Fungus looked miserable as he sat chewing his deer meat. He was fed up of everyone thinking that his weedy wimp of a brother was a hero. He'd show them, he thought. He could be a hero if he wanted, *and* he could catch a mammoth. Yes, he'd show them. When the time was right, he would be ready...

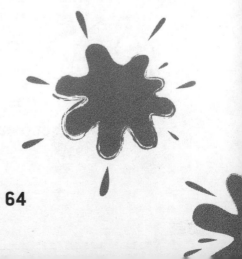